Here's what kids have to say to
Mary Pope Osborne, author of
the Magic Tree House series:

*I wish I could keep all your books in a glass
case with a golden key.*—Luke R.

*I love your books because they are funny
and scary.*—Michael C.

I'd like to be a writer just like you.
—Meghan G.

*I hope you come out with more than one
hundred Jack and Annie books.*—Brock G.

Your books really make me dream.—Kurt K.

*I think you are the best writer in all
mankind!*—Heather O.

Write to Mary Pope Osborne yourself!
See the last page for the address.

Look for these books by
Mary Pope Osborne!

Magic Tree House books:
Dinosaurs Before Dark (#1)
The Knight at Dawn (#2)
Mummies in the Morning (#3)
Pirates Past Noon (#4)
Night of the Ninjas (#5)
Afternoon on the Amazon (#6)
Sunset of the Sabertooth (#7)

Picture books:
Molly and the Prince
Moonhorse

For middle-grade readers:
American Tall Tales
Best Wishes, Joe Brady
Run, Run, as Fast as You Can
*Spider Kane and the Mystery at
    Jumbo Nightcrawler's*
*Spider Kane and the Mystery Under
    the May-Apple*

Magic Tree House #6

Afternoon on the Amazon

by Mary Pope Osborne

illustrated by Sal Murdocca

Random House New York

For Piers Pope Boyce

Text copyright © 1995 by Mary Pope Osborne.
Illustrations copyright © 1995 by Sal Murdocca.
All rights reserved under International and Pan-American
Copyright Conventions. Published in the United States by
Random House, Inc., New York, and simultaneously in Canada
by Random House of Canada Limited, Toronto.

Library of Congress Cataloging-in-Publication Data
Osborne, Mary Pope. Afternoon on the Amazon / by Mary Pope Osborne ;
illustrated by Sal Murdocca.
    p. cm. — (The Magic tree house series ; #6) "A First stepping stone book."
SUMMARY: Eight-year-old Jack, his seven-year-old sister, Annie, and Peanut
the mouse ride in a tree house to the Amazon rain forest, where they encounter
flesh-eating piranhas, hungry crocodiles, and wild jaguars.
ISBN 0-679-86372-9 (pbk.) — ISBN 0-679-96372-3 (lib. bdg.)
[1. Rain forests—Fiction. 2. Rain forest animals—Fiction. 3. Adventure and
adventures—Fiction. 4. Tree houses—Fiction. 5. Amazon River Valley—Fiction.]
I. Murdocca, Sal, ill. II. Title. III. Series: Osborne, Mary Pope. Magic tree house
series ; #6.
PZ7.O81167Af   1995
[Fic]—dc20   95-3237

Manufactured in the United States of America

Random House, Inc.   New York, Toronto, London, Sydney, Auckland

20 19 18 17 16 15 14 13 12 11

Contents

Afternoon
on the
Amazon

Prologue

One summer day in Frog Creek, Pennsylvania, a mysterious tree house appeared in the woods.

Eight-year-old Jack and his seven-year-old sister, Annie, climbed into the tree house. They found it was filled with books.

Jack and Annie soon discovered that the tree house was magic. It could take them to the places in the books. All they had to do was to point to a picture and wish to go there.

Jack and Annie visited the times of

dinosaurs, knights, pyramids, pirates, and ninjas. Along the way, they discovered that the tree house belongs to Morgan le Fay. Morgan is a magical librarian from the time of King Arthur. She travels through time and space, gathering books.

In their last adventure, *Night of the Ninjas*, Jack and Annie learned that Morgan was under a spell. To free her, Jack and Annie have to find four special things.

In old Japan, they found the first thing: a moonstone.

Now Jack and Annie are about to set out in search of the second thing...in *Afternoon on the Amazon*.

2

1

Where's Peanut?

"Hurry, Jack!" shouted Annie.

Annie ran into the Frog Creek woods.

Jack followed her.

"It's still here!" Annie called.

Jack caught up with Annie. She stood beside a tall oak tree.

Jack looked up. The magic tree house was shining in the afternoon sunlight.

"We're coming, Peanut!" Annie called.

She grabbed the rope ladder and started up.

Jack followed. They climbed and climbed. Finally they climbed into the tree house.

"Peanut?" said Annie.

Jack took off his backpack. He looked around.

Sunlight slanted across a stack of books—books about ninjas, pirates, mummies, knights, and dinosaurs.

The letter M shimmered on the wooden floor. M for Morgan le Fay.

"I don't think Peanut's here," said Jack.

"I wonder where she is," said Annie.

"How do you know Peanut's a *she?*" asked Jack.

"I just know it," said Annie.

"Oh, brother," said Jack.

Squeak!

Annie laughed. "Look, Jack!"

A small pink sock was moving across the

4

floor. Yesterday Annie had turned her sock
into a bed for Peanut.

Annie picked up the tiny lump.

Squeak.

A brown-and-white mouse peeked out of the sock. She looked from Annie to Jack with her big eyes.

Jack laughed. "Hi, Peanut," he said.

"Will you help us again today?" asked Annie.

In old Japan, Peanut had helped them when they'd gotten lost.

"We have to find three more things for Morgan," said Annie.

Jack pushed his glasses into place. "First we have to find a clue that tells us where to begin," he said.

"Guess what," said Annie.

"What?" said Jack.

"We don't have to look very far." She pointed at a corner of the tree house.

In the shadows was an open book.

2

Big Bugs

"Wow," said Jack, picking up the book. "The ninja book was open yesterday. Now this one. Who opened them?"

Jack closed the book and looked at the cover.

It showed a picture of a green forest. The trees were very tall and close together.

On the cover were the words *The Rain Forest*.

"Oh, wow," said Jack.

"Oh, no," said Annie.

"What's wrong?" said Jack.

"I learned about the rain forest in school," said Annie. "It's filled with big bugs and spiders."

"I know," said Jack. "Half of them have never even been named."

"It's creepy," said Annie.

"It's neat," said Jack. He wanted to take lots of notes in the rain forest. Maybe he could even name some unknown bugs.

"Neat? Yuk," said Annie. She shivered.

"I don't get it," said Jack. "You weren't afraid of dinosaurs."

"So?"

"You weren't afraid of the castle guards or the mummy's ghost."

"So?"

"You weren't afraid of pirates or ninjas."

"So?"

"You're not afraid of *really* scary things. But you're afraid of little bugs and spiders. That doesn't make sense."

"So?"

Jack sighed. "Listen," he said. "We have to go there. To help Morgan. That's why the book was left open."

"I know that," said Annie, frowning.

"Plus, the rain forests are being cut down," said Jack. "Don't you want to see one before it's too late?"

Annie took a deep breath and slowly nodded.

"Okay, then, let's go," said Jack.

He opened the book again. He pointed to a picture that showed blue sky, green leaves, and bright flowers.

"I wish we could go there," he said.

The wind began to blow.

Squeak.

"Stay here, Peanut," said Annie as she put the mouse in her pocket.

The wind picked up. The tree house started to spin.

Jack squeezed his eyes shut.

The wind was whistling now. The tree house was spinning faster and faster.

Then everything was still.

Absolutely still.

Wild sounds broke the silence.

Screeeeeech!

Buzzzzzzz!

Chirp! Chirp!

3

Yikes!

Jack opened his eyes.

The air was hot and steamy.

"It looks like we landed in some bushes," said Annie.

She was peeking out of the tree house window. Peanut was peeking out of Annie's pocket.

Jack peeked out of the tree house, too.

They had landed in a sea of shiny green leaves. Outside there were flowers, bright butterflies, and birds. Just as in the book.

"That's strange," said Jack. "I wonder

why we didn't land in a tree. The way we always do."

"I don't know," said Annie. "But let's hurry and find the thing for Morgan. So we can get back home before we meet any big bugs."

"Wait. This seems weird," said Jack. "I don't understand why we landed in bushes. I'd better read about this."

"Oh, come on," said Annie. "We don't even need the ladder. We can just climb out the window."

Annie put Peanut in her pocket. She stuck one leg out the window.

"Wait!" Jack grabbed Annie's other leg. He read:

The rain forest is in three layers.
Thick treetops, often over 150 feet

in the air, make up the top layer.
This is called the forest canopy.
Below the canopy is the under-
story, then the forest floor.

"Get back in here!" cried Jack. "We're
probably more than 150 feet above the
ground! In the forest canopy!"

"Yikes!" said Annie. She slipped back into the tree house.

"We *have* to use the ladder," said Jack. He got on his hands and knees. He moved leaves away from the hole in the floor. He looked down.

The ladder seemed to fall between the branches of a giant tree. But Jack couldn't see beyond that.

"I can't tell what's down there," he said. "Be careful."

Jack put the rain forest book in his backpack. Then he stepped onto the rope ladder.

He started down. Annie followed with Peanut in her pocket.

Jack pushed through the leaves.

He came to the understory below the canopy.

He looked down at the forest floor. It was very far away.

"Oh, man," whispered Jack.

This world was completely different from the one above the treetops.

Now that they were out of the sun, it was cooler. It was also damp and very quiet.

Jack shivered. It was the spookiest place he had ever seen.

4

Millions of Them!

Jack didn't move. He kept staring down at the forest floor.

"What's wrong?" Annie called from above.

Jack didn't answer.

"You don't see any giant spiders, do you?" Annie said.

"Well...no." Jack took a deep breath.

We have to keep going, he thought. We have to find the special thing for Morgan.

"No spiders. Nothing scary," Jack called. And he started down the ladder again.

Jack and Annie climbed down through the

understory. Finally they stepped onto the forest floor.

Only a few rays of light slanted through the gloom.

The trees were very, very tall and very wide. Vines and moss were hanging everywhere. The ground was covered with dead leaves.

"Before we do anything, I'd better check the book," said Jack.

He pulled out the rain forest book. He found a picture of the dark world under the treetops.

He read:

In the rain forest, many living creatures blend in with their surroundings. This is called camouflage.

"Oh, man," said Jack. He closed the book and looked around. "There're *tons* of creatures down here. We just can't see them."

"Really?" whispered Annie.

She and Jack peered around at the quiet forest. Jack felt unseen eyes watching them.

"Let's hurry and find the special thing," whispered Annie.

"How will we know when we find it?" Jack said.

"I think we'll just know," said Annie. She headed off through the gloom.

Jack followed. They crept between the huge trees and past hanging vines.

Annie stopped. "Wait—what's that?"

"What's what?"

"Listen—that weird sound."

Jack listened. He heard a crackling sound.

It sounded like a person walking over leaves.

Jack looked around. He didn't see anyone.

But the sound got louder.

Was it an animal? A giant bug? One that had never been named?

Just then the silent forest came alive.

Birds took off into the air. Frogs hopped over the leaves. Lizards ran up the tree trunks.

The weird noise grew louder and louder.

"Maybe the book explains it," said Jack. He opened the book. He found a picture of different animals running together. He read:

When animals hear a crackling sound, they flee in panic. The sound means that 30 million flesh-eating army ants are marching through the dead leaves.

"It's army ants!" cried Jack. "Millions of them!"

"Where?" cried Annie.

Jack and Annie looked around wildly.

"There!" Annie pointed.

Army ants—millions and millions of them—were marching over the leaves!

"Run to the tree house!" cried Annie.

"Where is it?" said Jack, whirling around. All the trees looked the same. Where was the rope ladder?

"Just run!" cried Annie.

Jack and Annie took off.

They ran over the dead leaves.

They ran between wide tree trunks.

They ran past the hanging vines and mosses.

They climbed over thick roots.

Jack saw a clearing ahead. It was filled with sunlight.

"That way!" he cried.

Jack and Annie hurried toward the light. They pushed their way through the bushes.

They burst onto the bank of a river.

They stared at the slow-moving brown water.

"Do you think the ants will come this way?" Annie said, panting.

"I don't know," said Jack. "But if we wade a few feet into the river, we're safe. The ants won't go into the water. Come on."

"Look!" said Annie.

She pointed to a big log rocking at the edge of the river. The inside of the log was dug out.

"It looks like a canoe," said Jack. He listened to the crackling sound in the distance. "Let's get in it. Quick!"

Jack shoved the book into his backpack. Then he and Annie carefully climbed into the dug-out log.

Annie leaned out of it. She pushed away from the bank with her hands.

"Wait!" said Jack. "We don't have paddles!"

"Oops," said Annie.

The canoe started moving slowly down the muddy river.

5
Pretty Fish

Squeak.

Annie patted the little mouse in her pocket.

"It's okay, Peanut. The ants can't get us in the river. We're safe," she said.

"Maybe safe from the ants," said Jack. "But where is this canoe going?"

Jack and Annie stared at the river. Branches spread over the water. Vines and mosses hung down from them.

"We'd better look this up," said Jack. He pulled the rain forest book out of his backpack and flipped through it.

Soon he found a picture of a river. He read:

The Amazon River stretches over 4,000 miles from the mountains of Peru, across Brazil, to the Atlantic Ocean. The river basin contains over half of the rain forests in the world.

Jack looked at Annie. "We're on the Amazon River," he said. "It's more than four thousand miles long!"

"Wow," Annie whispered. She looked at the river. She trailed her hand through the water.

"I have to make some notes—" Jack said. He pulled his notebook out of his pack. He wrote:

The Amazon rain forest is

"Jack, look at those pretty fish with the teeth," said Annie.

"What?" Jack glanced up from his writing.

Annie was pointing at some blue fish swimming near the boat. The fish had red bellies and razor-sharp teeth.

"Watch it!" cried Jack. "Those aren't pretty fish. They're piranhas! They'll eat anything! Even people!"

"Yikes," whispered Annie.

"We better get back on shore," said Jack, putting the books in his backpack.

"How?" said Annie. "We can't go in the water now. And we don't have any paddles."

Jack tried to stay calm. "We need a plan," he said.

Jack stared at the river. The canoe would soon float under some vines.

"I'll grab a vine," said Jack. "And pull us to shore."

"Good idea," said Annie.

As they glided under the branches, Jack stood up.

The canoe rocked. He nearly fell out.

"Balance the canoe," said Jack.

Annie leaned to one side. Jack reached—
he missed!

The canoe floated under more branches.

Jack reached for another thick vine.

He grabbed it!

It was cold and scaly. It wiggled and
jerked!

"*Ahhh!*" Jack screamed and fell back into the canoe.

The vine was alive!

It was a long green snake!

The snake fell from the tree. It splashed into the water and swam away.

"Oh, man," said Jack.

He and Annie stared in horror at each other.

"What now?" said Annie, making a face.

"Well..." Jack looked at the river. There were no vines up ahead. But there was a big branch floating on the water.

"Grab that branch near you," said Jack. "Maybe we can use it for a paddle."

The canoe floated closer to the branch. Annie reached for it.

Suddenly the branch rose into the air!

It was a *crocodile!*

"Help!" screamed Annie, and she fell back into the canoe.

The crocodile opened and closed its huge, long jaws. Then it moved past the canoe and swam up the river.

"Oh, man," whispered Jack.

A screeching sound split the air.

Jack and Annie jumped.

"Help!" said Jack.

He expected to see another terrible creature.

But all he saw was a small brown monkey, hanging by its tail from a tree.

6

Monkey Trouble

Squeak! Squeak! Peanut poked her head out from Annie's pocket. She seemed to be yelling at the monkey.

"Don't worry, Peanut," said Annie. "He's just a little monkey. He won't hurt us."

But suddenly the monkey grabbed a big red fruit hanging from the tree. He hurled it at the canoe.

"Watch it!" shouted Jack.

The fruit fell into the water with a splash.

The monkey screeched even louder.

He grabbed another fruit.

"Don't throw things at us!" shouted Annie.

But the monkey hurled the red fruit right at them.

Jack and Annie ducked again. And the fruit splashed into the water.

"Stop that!" Annie shouted.

But the monkey only waved his arms and screeched again.

"Oh, brother," said Jack. "I don't believe this."

The monkey grabbed a third fruit and hurled it at Jack and Annie. It landed inside the canoe with a thump.

Annie grabbed the fruit. She stood up and threw it back at the monkey.

She missed. The canoe rocked. Annie almost fell out.

The monkey screeched even louder.

"Go away!" Annie shouted. "You're the meanest thing in the world!"

The monkey stopped screeching.

He looked at Annie. Then he swung away. Into the forest.

"I think I hurt his feelings," said Annie.

"Who cares?" said Jack. "He shouldn't throw things."

"Uh-oh," said Annie. "It's raining now."

"What?" Jack looked up. A raindrop hit him in the eye.

"Oh, no. I don't believe this," Jack said.

"What'd you expect?" said Annie. "It *is* the *rain* forest."

A gust of wind blew the canoe.

Thunder rolled in the sky.

"A river's a bad place to be in a storm,"

said Jack. "We have to get back to shore. Right now."

"But how?" said Annie. "We can't wade or swim. The piranhas, the snake, and the crocodile will get us."

Screeching split the air again.

"Oh, no," said Jack. The bratty monkey was back.

This time, the monkey was pointing a long stick at the canoe.

Jack crouched down. Was the monkey going to hurl the stick at them? Like a spear?

Annie jumped up and faced the monkey.

"Watch it! He's nuts," said Jack.

But the monkey just stared at Annie. And Annie just stared back at him.

After a long moment, the monkey seemed to smile.

Annie smiled back.

"What's going on?" said Jack.

"He wants to help us," Annie said.

"Help us how?" said Jack.

The monkey held out the long stick.

Annie grabbed the other end.

The monkey pulled on the stick. The canoe started floating toward him.

The monkey pulled the canoe all the way to the bank of the river.

7

Freeze!

Jack and Annie jumped out of the canoe.

The rain was starting to fall harder.

The monkey took off. He swung from tree to tree, heading up the riverbank.

He screeched and beckoned to Jack and Annie.

"He wants us to follow him!" said Annie.

"No! We have to find the special thing. Then go home!" said Jack.

"He wants to help us!" said Annie. She took off after the monkey.

The two of them vanished into the rain forest.

"Annie!"

Thunder shook the sky.

"Oh, brother," said Jack.

He dashed after Annie and the monkey. Into the dark forest.

The forest seemed surprisingly dry.

Jack looked up. It was still raining. But the treetops acted like a huge umbrella.

"Annie?" called Jack.

"Jack! Jack!" cried Annie.

"Where are you?"

"Here!"

Jack hurried in the direction of Annie's voice.

Soon he found the monkey. He was screeching and swinging from a tree.

41

Annie was kneeling on the forest floor. She was playing with an animal that looked like a giant kitten.

"What's that?" Jack said.

"I don't know, but I love it!" said Annie.

Annie batted the animal's paws. It had gold fur and black spots.

"I'd better find out what it is," said Jack. He pulled out the rain forest book and flipped through it.

"Oh, it's so cute," said Annie.

Jack found a picture of an animal with gold fur and black spots. He read:

The jaguar is the biggest predator in the western hemisphere.

"Forget cute," Jack said. "That must be a baby jaguar. It's going to grow up and be the biggest predator in—"

"What's a predator?" asked Annie.

GRRR! There was a terrible growl.

Jack whirled around.

The mother jaguar was coming out from behind a tree. She was creeping over the dead leaves—*right toward Annie.*

"Freeze!" whispered Jack.

Annie froze. But the jaguar kept moving slowly toward her.

"Help," said Jack weakly.

Suddenly the monkey swooped down from his tree. He grabbed the jaguar's tail!

The cat roared and spun around.

Annie jumped up.

The monkey pulled the jaguar's tail again. Then he let go and took off.

The jaguar sprang after him.

"Run, Annie!" cried Jack.

Jack and Annie took off through the rain forest. They ran for their lives!

8

Vampire Bats?

"Wait—" said Jack, panting. "I think we got away."

Jack and Annie stopped running and caught their breath.

"Where are we?" said Jack.

"Where's the monkey?" said Annie, looking back at the forest. "Do you think the jaguar caught him?"

"No, monkeys are fast," said Jack.

Of course, jaguars are fast, too, Jack thought. But he didn't want to tell Annie that.

"I hope he's okay," said Annie.

Squeak. Peanut peeked out of Annie's pocket.

"Peanut! I almost forgot you!" said Annie. "Are you okay?"

The mouse just stared at Annie with her big eyes.

"She looks scared," said Jack. "Poor Peanut."

"Poor monkey," said Annie. She looked around at the forest.

"We'd better check the book," Jack said.

He pulled out the book. He turned the pages, searching for help.

He stopped at a picture of a scary creature.

"Oh, man. What's this?" he said.

Jack read the writing below the picture. It said:

Vampire bats live in the Amazon rain forest. At night, they quietly bite their victims and suck their blood.

"Vampire bats?" said Jack. He felt faint.

"Vampire bats?" said Annie.

Jack nodded. "After dark."

Annie and Jack looked around. The rain forest seemed to be getting even darker.

"Yikes," said Annie. She looked at Jack. "Maybe we should go home."

Jack nodded. For once he agreed with her.

"But what about our mission?" said Annie. "What about Morgan?"

"We'll come back," said Jack. "We'll have to be prepared."

"So we'll come back tomorrow?" Annie asked.

"Right. Now which way is the tree house?" said Jack.

"This way," said Annie, pointing.

"That way," said Jack, pointing in the opposite direction.

They looked at each other. "We're lost," they said together.

Squeak.

"Don't worry, Peanut." Annie started to pat the mouse again. But then she stopped.

Squeak. Squeak. Squeak.

"Jack, I think Peanut wants to help us," said Annie.

"How?"

"The way she helped us in the time of ninjas—"

Annie placed the mouse on the leafy forest floor. "Take us to the tree house, Peanut."

The mouse took off.

"Where'd she go?" said Annie. "I don't see her!"

"There!" said Jack. He pointed to leaves rustling on the ground.

A streak of white passed over the leaves.

"Yes, there!" said Annie.

Jack and Annie followed the moving leaves. The streak of white appeared. And disappeared.

Suddenly Jack stopped.

The forest floor was still. There was no sign of Peanut.

"Where is she?" asked Jack.

He kept staring at the ground.

"Jack!"

Jack glanced around. Annie was standing on the other side of a nearby tree. She was pointing up.

Jack looked up.

The tree house.

"Oh, whew," Jack said softly.

"She saved us again," said Annie. "She's running up the ladder. All by herself. Look."

Annie pointed at the rope ladder.

Peanut was climbing up one of the ropes.

"Let's go," Jack said.

Annie started up the ladder. Then Jack.

They followed Peanut all the way up to the canopy of the rain forest.

9

The Thing

Jack and Annie climbed into the tree house.

Peanut was sitting on a stack of books.

Annie patted Peanut's little head. "Thanks," she said softly.

"I have to write some notes about the rain forest," said Jack. "You find the Pennsylvania book."

Annie began searching for the Pennsylvania book—the book that always took them home.

Jack pulled out his notebook.

He had wanted to take lots of notes here.
But all he'd written so far was:

The Amazon rain forest is

"It's not here!" said Annie.

"What?" Jack looked up. He glanced around the tree house.

Annie was right. The Pennsylvania book was nowhere in sight.

"Was it here before we left home?" said Jack.

"I don't remember," said Annie.

"Oh, man," said Jack. "Now we can't get back to Frog Creek."

"That means we'll be here when the vampire bats come out," said Annie.

Something came flying through the tree house window.

"Ahhh!" Jack and Annie hid their heads.

Thud.

Something hit the floor. A red fruit.

Jack looked up. The monkey was sitting in the window. His head was cocked to one side. He seemed to be grinning at them.

"You're safe!" said Annie.

"Thanks for saving us," said Jack.

The monkey just grinned.

"I have just one question," said Annie. She pointed at the fruit. "Why do you keep throwing those at us?"

The monkey grabbed the fruit.

"No! Don't throw it!" said Jack. He ducked.

But the monkey didn't throw the fruit.

He held it out to Annie. He moved his lips as if he were trying to say something.

Annie stared into the monkey's eyes. He moved his lips again.

"Wow," Annie said softly. "I understand now."

"Understand what?" said Jack.

Annie took the fruit from the monkey. "This is it," she said. "The *thing* we need."

"What thing?" said Jack.

"One of the special things we're supposed to find for Morgan," Annie said. "To free her from the spell."

"Are you sure?" said Jack.

Before Annie could answer, Jack saw the Pennsylvania book. "Look! Our book!" he said, pointing.

"We found the thing. And now we can see the book," said Annie. "That's the way it works, remember?"

Jack nodded. Now he remembered. The ninja master said they wouldn't be able to find the Pennsylvania book until they had found what they were looking for.

The monkey screeched with laughter.

Jack and Annie looked at him. He was clapping his hands together.

Annie laughed with him. "How did you know to give this to us?" she said. "Who told you to do that?"

The monkey just waved at Jack and Annie. Then he turned and swung away out of the tree house.

"Wait!" said Jack, looking out the window.

Too late.

The monkey was gone. He had vanished below the treetops.

"Good-bye!" called Annie.

A happy screech came from the mysterious world below.

Jack sighed. He picked up his notebook again. He looked at his writing:

The Amazon vain forest is

He had to write *something* before they left. He quickly added—

amazing

Jack put away his notebook. Annie picked up the Pennsylvania book.

"Now it's really time to leave," she said.

She turned to the picture of the Frog Creek woods. "I wish we could go there," she said, pointing at the picture.

The wind started to blow.
The leaves began to tremble.
The tree house began to spin.
It spun faster and faster.
Then everything was still.
Absolutely still.

10

Halfway There

Squeak.

Jack opened his eyes. Peanut was on the tree house windowsill.

"We're home," said Annie.

Jack breathed a sigh of relief.

Annie held the fruit up to the afternoon light.

"What exactly *is* this?" she asked.

"Maybe it's in the book," Jack answered.

He pulled out the rain forest book. He flipped through the pages. He came to a picture of the red fruit.

"Here it is!" he said. He read out loud:

"The mango has a sweet taste like that of a peach."

"Mango? Hmmm," said Annie. She brought the fruit close to her lips.

"Hey!" said Jack, grabbing the mango from her. "We have to put it with the moonstone."

Jack placed the mango on the M carved into the floor. Next to the clear moonstone.

"Moonstone...mango," whispered Annie. It sounded like a spell.

"We're halfway there," said Jack. "Two more to go."

"Then we can free you, Morgan!" Annie called, as if Morgan were nearby.

"How do you know she can hear you?" said Jack.

"I just feel it," Annie said.

"Oh, brother," said Jack. He needed more proof than that.

Squeak. Peanut was looking at Jack and Annie.

"We have to leave you now," Jack said to the mouse.

Squeak.

"Can't we take her with us?" said Annie.

"No," said Jack. "Mom won't let us keep a mouse in the house. She doesn't like mice, remember?"

"How could anyone *not* like a mouse?" said Annie.

Jack smiled. "How could anyone not like a spider?" he said.

"That's different." Annie patted Peanut's head. "Bye," she said. "Wait for us here. We'll be back tomorrow."

Jack patted the mouse, too. "Bye, Peanut. Thanks for your help," he said.

Squeak.

Jack put the rain forest book on top of the book about ninjas.

Then he pulled on his backpack. And he and Annie left the tree house.

They climbed down the rope ladder. They stepped onto the ground.

They started walking through the Frog Creek woods.

Leaf shadows danced in the light.

A bird called out.

These woods are very different from the rain forest, Jack thought.

"There're no jaguars or army ants here," he said. "No little monkeys."

"You know, that monkey was never being mean," said Annie. "He was just trying to give us the mango."

"I know. Actually, nothing was being *mean*," said Jack. "The army ants were just marching. That's what army ants do."

"The piranhas were just being piranhas," said Annie.

"The snake was just being a snake," said Jack.

"The crocodile was just being a crocodile," said Annie.

"The jaguar was just taking care of her baby," said Jack.

Annie shuddered. "I still don't love bugs," she said.

"You don't have to *love* them," said Jack.

"Just leave them alone. And they won't bother you."

In fact, that's true about the whole rain forest, Jack thought. Everyone should just leave it all alone.

"Who cares if the bugs don't have names?" he said softly. "*They* know who they are."

Jack and Annie stepped out of the Frog Creek woods.

They started walking up their street. It was lit with a golden light.

"Race you!" said Annie.

They took off running.

They ran across their yard.

They raced up their steps.

"Safe!" they shouted together, tagging their front door.

Where have *you* traveled in the
MAGIC TREE HOUSE?

The Mystery of the Tree House
(Books #1–4)

❏ **Magic Tree House #1, Dinosaurs Before Dark,**
in which Jack and Annie discover the tree house and
travel back to the time of dinosaurs.

❏ **Magic Tree House #2, The Knight at Dawn,**
in which Jack and Annie go to the time of knights
and explore a medieval castle with a hidden passage.

❏ **Magic Tree House #3, Mummies in the Morning,**
in which Jack and Annie go to ancient Egypt and get
lost in a pyramid when they help a ghost queen.

❏ **Magic Tree House #4, Pirates Past Noon,**
in which Jack and Annie travel back in time and meet
some unfriendly pirates searching for buried treasure.

The Mystery of the Magic Spell
(Books #5–8)

❑ **Magic Tree House #5, NIGHT OF THE NINJAS,** in which Jack and Annie go to old Japan and learn the secrets of the ninjas.

❑ **Magic Tree House #6, AFTERNOON ON THE AMAZON,** in which Jack and Annie explore the wild rain forest of the Amazon and are greeted by giant ants, hungry crocodiles, and flesh-eating piranhas.

❑ **Magic Tree House #7, SUNSET OF THE SABERTOOTH,** in which Jack and Annie go back to the Ice Age—the world of woolly mammoths, sabertooth tigers, and a mysterious sorcerer.

❑ **Magic Tree House #8, MIDNIGHT ON THE MOON,** in which Jack and Annie go forward in time to a space station on the moon, where they ride in a moon buggy and have a close encounter with a moon man.